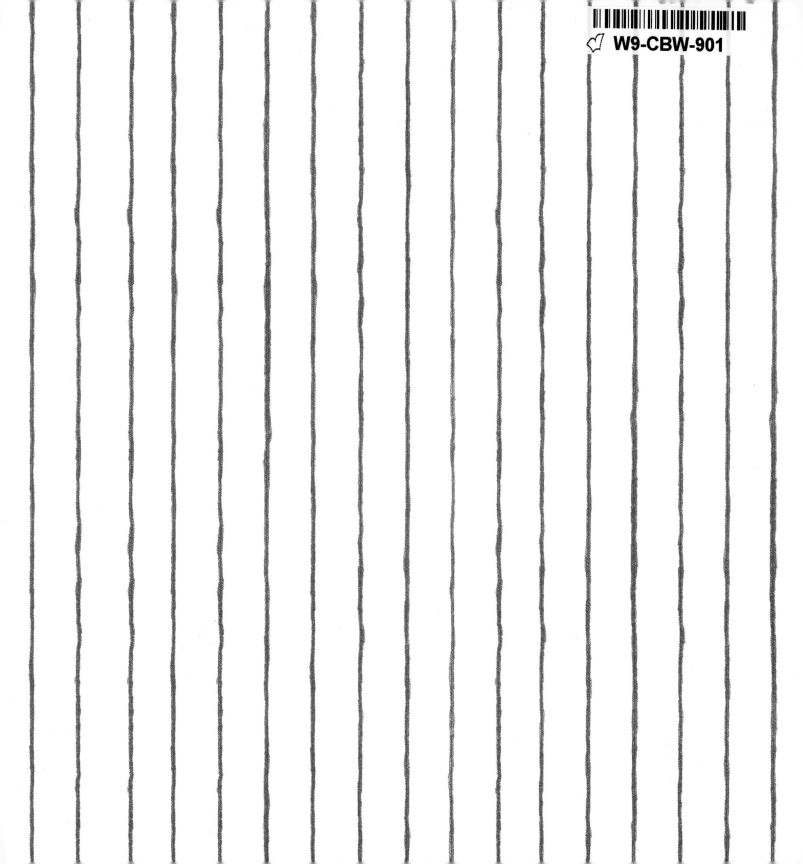

# BALLPARK

by
**Eileen R. Meyer**

illustrated by
**Carlynn Whitt**

two lions

For the all-stars in my life—Keith, William,
Christian, and Mitchell. And for my father,
who instilled a love of sports in me.   —E.R.M.

For my boys.   —C.W.

GO TEAM

two lions

Text copyright © 2014 Eileen R. Meyer
Illustrations copyright © 2014 Carlynn Whitt
All rights reserved.

Published by TWO LIONS, NEW YORK

www.apub.com

Library of Congress Cataloging-in-Publication Data
available upon request.

ISBN-13: 9781477847190
ISBN-10: 1477847197

The illustrations were rendered in in traditional
mixed media and Photoshop.

Book design by Vera Soki

Printed in China (R)
First edition

It's our big day—
just us two.
We have our gloves,
and mine's brand new.

There's the ballpark,
big and wide.
Let's hurry up
and go inside!

There's the field!
Men stretch and run.
They sign for fans
before they're done.

Our team's in pinstripes.
They're in gray.
We hope our team
will win today.

We see the flag.
It waves up high.
We sing a song
and watch it fly.

The teams are ready
for the call.
The umpire shouts out,

LET'S PLAY BALL!

What if a foul ball
comes right here?
I'll make the play,
and you can cheer!

# CRACK!

The shortstop
jumps—line drive.
He caught the ball!
We both high-five.

# GET PEANUTS HERE!

the vendor yells.
We share a bag
and crack the shells.

WHACK!

The ball sails
through the air.
It's down the line
and bounces fair.

A runner steals.
He slides in low.
We whoop and shout—
he beats the throw!

The crowd stands up.
The players rest.
We sing and stretch.
Our team's the best.

A swing, then

A high fly ball.
We squint and watch it
clear the wall.

The game is over.
Our team won!
We sang and cheered.
We had some fun!

And next year we
can come back, too . . .
just you with me
and me with you!